MARSHA IS MAGNETIC

Text by
Beth Ferry

Illustrations by
Lorena Alvarez

HOUGHTON MIFFLIN HARCOURT
Boston   New York

For the real Marsha —B.F.
For my Dad, Florencio —L.A.

hmhbooks.com

The illustrations for this book were sketched and colored using Procreate.
The text type was set in Interstate.
The display type was hand lettered by Lorena Alvarez.

Designed by Whitney Leader-Picone

Library of Congress Cataloging-in-Publication data is on file.

ISBN: 978-0-544-73584-2

Manufactured in China
SCP 10 9 8 7 6 5 4 3 2 1
4500809166

MARSHA was a scientist with a problem.
  A Big Problem.
  A Big Birthday Party Problem.

Although *she* knew that birthdays were just the measure of the Earth's rotation around the Sun, *other* people had *other* ideas.

Her mom was in full party mode: decorating the walls, making the piñata, baking, and smiling and skipping around the house.

"Don't forget to hand out the invitations,"
her mom sang.
Thus, the Big Birthday Party Problem.

There was only one solution.

THE SCIENTIFIC METHOD

1. Make an Observation.
2. Ask a Question.
3. Formulate a Hypothesis.
4. Test the Hypothesis.
5. Analyze Data.
6. Make a Conclusion.

Cards

Party Hats

$A = \frac{1}{2} \cdot a \cdot \frac{2\pi r \cdot g}{2} = \pi r g$

CAKE:

FLOUR

MUSIC
•Playlist

★MY PARTY!

THINGS I NEED:
•Balloons
•a Cake!
•Music
•Friends!

STEP 1: OBSERVE

At school the next day,
Marsha observed Christa.

She noted her study habits, sports skills, hairstyles, and clothing choices.

But no matter how she sorted the data, she could not figure it out.

"Why is she popular?" Marsha mused.

"Kids are just naturally drawn to her," her mother answered.

Kids were not drawn to Marsha.
Oh, sometimes they *drew* her.
She was pretty easy to sketch, with copper curls and owl glasses. Most kids drew a pretty good likeness, but as for LIKING her, well, not so much.

Marsha's scientific experiments repelled people: growing mold, studying slime, keeping rats as pets.

STEP 2: QUESTION

"How does Christa have so many friends?" Marsha asked.

"Maybe she has a great sense of humor," her dad said. "Or a magnetic personality."

Of course, Marsha thought. *That's it!*

STEP 3:
HYPOTHESIS

So Marsha did what any good scientist would do—she ordered supplies. Overnight delivery.

When her package arrived, she went right to work.
She hammered and pounded and coiled and plugged.
She measured and glued and stapled.

Soon her creation was finished.
And it was **PERFECT!**

When Marsha came down the next morning, her mother said, "My, my, don't you look . . . attractive."

"**I FEEL ATTRACTIVE**," Marsha answered.

She sat down and *clank*, the spoon flew toward her.

She pried it off and tried again. *Clank.*

"I'll just have bread," she said, keeping clear of the refrigerator . . . and the toaster.

As she walked through the kitchen, objects flew toward her . . . and stuck.

"Do you have anything to tell me?" her mother asked.

"No, Mom. Just planning on a great day."

STEP 4: TESTING

Marsha walked confidently down the hall.
Within seconds, Amy zoomed toward her.

"Hi!" Marsha said.
"I think I'm stuck to you," Amy replied.
"Perfect!" said Marsha. "Let's walk to class together."

As they walked, Marsha noticed Amy's earrings.

"Do you like cupcakes?"

"They're my favorite," said Amy.

"Mine too," said Marsha. "Did you know that baking cupcakes requires a chemical reaction?"

"That's . . . cool," Amy said.

Marsha handed her an invitation.

"Cupcakes at my house this weekend?"

"Um, sure," said Amy.

Marsha beamed.

As they walked, more and more kids
stuck to Marsha.
By their watches and bracelets.
Through their backpacks and belts.
Marsha tucked and tied invitations
to everyone she could reach.

A sculpture of
students tumbled
into the art room.

STEP 5: DATA

Mr. Allen sorted everyone out . . .
by physically pulling them off Marsha.

Marsha quickly sorted the data.
Her dress was a **SUCCESS!**

At the end of class, Marsha tried to get up.
But she was stuck tight.

As he tugged her free, Mr. Allen said,
"Maybe you should visit the nurse."

Marsha was late for gym, but no one seemed to notice.
"Problem?" Marsha asked.
"Mrs. Feeney lost the key. Now we can't have the kickball tournament."

Marsha knew just what to do.

She ran to the nurse and
retrieved her creation.

This time she plugged it in.
The magnet shivered and shook and hummed.
The door quivered and bucked and banged.

Finally, the doors burst open as the cart came charging through, flinging balls into the air.
Kids yelled and jumped and chased.
Marsha quietly unplugged her supermagnet and watched the hullabaloo.

But soon she found herself surrounded by cheering kids.

It was just the reaction she had hoped for.

Marsha's birthday party was positively wonderful.

She collected lots of data . . .
and presents . . . and even some
new friends.

And, at the end of the day, Marsha concluded
that the best way to make friends . . .

. . . was to just be herself.